CRY FOR MOTHER

J.E. ERICKSON

Paperback ISBN: 979-8-9869508-4-6

eBook ISBN: 979-8-9869508-5-3

-

Edited by 360 Editing

(a division of Uncomfortably Dark Horror)

Editors: Candace Nola. Darc Rose.

www.uncomfortablydark.com

-

Cover Design by Fabled Beast Design

Artist: A.A. Medina

www.fabledbeastdesign.wordpress.com

Other Books by J.E. Erickson

Offerings to the Flower Moon: The Tale of the Abrams Witch

Dust Bunnies From Hell

Always, in This Nightmare (Coming Feb 2024)

1

Crisp wind roared in Lance's ears and pressed against his body, a giant hand lowering him down to the checkerboard landscape of farms and lakes at terminal velocity.

A year ago, he'd be with Chris and Brandon, tumbling through the sky or standing up and hurtling downward like a human corkscrew, the tickle of the G-force squeezing his stomach and the freshest air a person could breathe filling his lungs and mixing with the blissful adrenaline in his bloodstream. It was his only drug.

Now he had nothing.

Last week, he went skydiving for the three hundredth time — but it was the first time he jumped without a parachute. Someone tried to tell him how long he free fell before his friend, Collin, scooped him up and floated them both to safety, but Lance didn't care. It wasn't long enough.

Scuba diving in an uncharted underwater cave was a birthday gift to himself, yet nobody had enough balls to come with him. "Dude, are you insane? How many people have died down there?" The entire experience ended up being for nothing. He found his way back without panicking or running short of air. It was fun, sure, but there was never any real danger. It's not like he ever got lost in the dark.

Rock climbing was boring and bungee jumping was for children. His shoulders were too broad for serious cave diving. Mountain boarding was fun for five minutes. Everything felt like a worn-out exercise routine. The last time he did anything remotely dangerous was with his motorcycle, and it ended with torn ribs and a hairline fracture to his femur. Even that wasn't exciting.

As he fell, Lance realized there was nothing he couldn't do. Nothing he couldn't live through. While other men were hitting 30 and winding down onto their flat, middle-aged asses and beer bellies from crushing donuts and hating their wives, he was a beast who bench pressed 400 pounds, ran a six-minute mile, and could pull any woman out of a bar in 60 seconds. Lance wasn't just at his peak; he was the peak. He had conquered fear. Death, injury, and rejection were afterthoughts. Nothing scared him.

Nothing.

Except the boredom. This soul crushing emptiness and ambivalence toward everything that he found fun gave him more of a stomachache than the shitty roller coasters at Six Flags that made kids and grown women scream. It gnawed at him. Bit at the edges of his patience like a nagging ex-girlfriend who wasn't satisfied with having the last word in an argument.

What the hell was the point? Not even 30 and he'd peaked. Done it all.

It'd almost be easier to just not pull the cord. Go out in a blaze. A nylon-clad falling star crashing into the earth an hour west of Minneapolis.

Lance waited until the other two pulled their chutes before pawing at his ripcord and releasing his red and gold parachute to put a miserable end to the free fall and begin the slow descent to the landing area.

"Dude, what's gnawing on your sac?" Brandon reclined in one of the bar's patio chairs and flicked the cap of his beer bottle at Lance. He missed.

"What do you mean?" Lance asked, trying to mask the irritation in his voice behind a smile and a swig of alcohol-free beer.

Collin ran a hand through his curly hair. "Yeah, Bran. What's up? Let the man bask in the afterglow of yet another bitchin jump."

Chris reached into the bucket of ice for another bottle. "In Brandon's defense, Lance has kinda been a pissy pants all day."

"Really? Pissy pants? What are we, eight years old?" Lance gave up hiding how sour he felt. There weren't many interesting looking women at the bar; a couple of sixes and a seven. The pretty server smiled at him twice already, but every woman did that. Maybe he'd get her number or take her to his place and fuck her later. Whatever. Even sex bored him.

"It's from a place of love, dude." Collin tipped his glass toward him.

"Yeah, man." Brandon dunked a crispy fried chicken leg into some honey mustard. Brown on brown. "Seriously. What's up?"

He wasn't about to talk about his feelings with these three, certainly not on the patio of a suburban dive bar. Good thing they were easily sidetracked. "How can you eat that shit, man?" The smell made Lance nauseous. "I tan that color."

Collin leaned closer to Brandon and faked a conspiratorial tone. "Lance's body is a temple."

"A temple to what?" Chris asked, clearly drunk. "Not like it's going to stop the worms from eating our dead asses."

Collin humored him with a nod, then turned back to Brandon. "Notice how he drinks the beer-flavored water but never the beer. Never had a drop of booze in his whole life." He laughed and clinked the ice around his glass of bourbon. "A straight-laced momma's boy."

"Hmmm." Brandon pointed at Lance with the chicken leg and matched Collin's tone. "But he eats chicken. As a matter of fact, I have heard shocking rumors that ninety percent of his protein intake is from our feathered fowl friends."

"He bakes them."

The metal table shook as Brandon sat up straight with an exaggerated gasp. "No! He doesn't take the skin off, too?"

Lance rolled his eyes. He could withstand their typical shit, but he didn't care to be the focus of conversation to-night. "The skin is the unhealthiest part. Best to just peel it away and toss it."

Brandon bit into the greasy leg and smacked his lips loud-ly. "But it's so good."

"You should have a vegetable."

"Mustard is a vegetable. I looked it up. So is peanut oil." Brandon ate like dog shit, but nobody could tell by his lanky frame; he ran half-marathons for fun. Every fat calorie probably burned away before the bar food hit his stomach.

"Peanuts aren't a vegetable," Chris said.

That's all it took to get them arguing back and forth like a couple of high school kids. In fifteen minutes, their arguments devolved into a tradeoff of 'Uh huh' and 'Nah ah' and at least one 'I know you are, but what am I.' None of it was serious, just bickering between friends. But did they have to be so childish? He was embarrassed for them.

They sipped their beers for another hour before Brandon and Chris left. They'd planned another jump the following morning before they'd head out to Utah for some camping and cave diving with Brandon's cousin, and they wanted to get an early start.

By the time they left, Lance had decided he'd fuck the server.

"You feel it too, huh?" Collin asked.

Lance blinked. Did he catch him staring at the server? "Feel what? The grease in the air from this lame ass bar? Why do you guys even like this place?"

Collin shrugged. "It's close, and the beer is cold. What's

not to like?" He downed his beer in one breath and spun the bottle on the table.

The two of them sat in silence as the last yellow hue of the sun sank past the horizon, pulling a trail of deep blue behind. Stars twinkled overhead. Even though they were in town, they were far enough away from the metro area's light pollution for the earliest stars to wake up and stretch their arms across the sky.

"Beautiful out." Collin leaned back; his chin pointed skyward. "I remember when I was a kid, up north on my grandpa's farm, how you could see the cloud of the Milky Way almost every night. And those few days every year when the northern lights came this far south. I used to sneak out into the soybean field and lay down in the dirt, just staring and wondering what the hell is up there." He lowered his gaze to Lance. "Ever do that? Wonder about greater things?"

Lance shook his head. Collin had better not be falling in with the Jesus freaks and bible thumpers who got a rush from spreading 'the good word' or however they were selling it now. That would mean one less friend. "Nah, man. There's nothing up there but empty space, gas, and trillions of tax dollars beaming cable television into your apartment and spying on Russians politicians or something. Besides, even if there was, we'd never get to it in this lifetime."

Collin made a soft laugh with his nose. A meaningful look darkened his green eyes. "You're bored, too, aren't you? With all of this? Life in general, maybe?"

Lance wasn't sure how to respond. Collin had been his friend since their freshman year of college, so he read Lance's moods pretty well. What Lance didn't want was to fall into one of Collin's long-winded speeches about opening himself up to alternative methods of feeding his need for a rush, speeches which almost always ended in a discussion of LSD or some other nonsense. The only drug Lance put in himself was caffeine. No booze, hardly any sugar. He didn't even smoke weed. And cigarettes and vapes were downright disgusting.

"It's cool, Lance. You don't have to say anything, man. I can tell. It's like numbness, right here." He put a fist into his stomach. "This constant reminder of jumping out of that first plane, or getting stuck in your first cave, but getting yourself out. When you're rock climbing forty, fifty feet in the air and your hand slips, and no matter how bad you're swinging, you take all of your weight onto the fingertips of your off-hand and keep your body steady. Grabbing so tight you become the mountain." He narrowed his eyes. "You know what I mean? That primitive understanding that only you can save you. When you know that no matter how close you can come to death, you'll always be the one to save you. To outsmart it. Outfight it."

Lance swallowed. Collin was spot on. He was also un-characteristically articulate. Lance wanted to doubt that he rehearsed it, but the suspicion nagged. "Who told you I was bored?"

"I can see it, man. Hell, I saw it last year when you didn't so much as smile when we BASE jumped the Golden Gate. How long did we hide while the cops searched? Five hours?"

"Six."

"Six hours, Lance. Man, I was shitting myself. But you, all you did was sit there, not even moving. No expression on your face." He laughed. "I bet if I went back in time and checked your pulse, it'd be steady."

Again, he was right. The butterflies somersaulted in his stomach when Collin was bullshitting their way into one of the bridge towers. He claimed they were construction workers going to check the tightness of this or that. But the jump felt routine — a four second fall and a twen-ty-second float. Once the secondary rush of avoiding po-lice wore off, numbness filled the void. Not even boredom. Just the absence of anything while watching boats, cars, and idiots search for them while they hid within the brush and rocks.

Collin leaned in. "Listen, I've got something. Something I've helped a few other people with." When Lance took a breath to speak, Collin held up his hand. "No drugs. Nothing like that. We talked about that, and I heard you."

"Good. That's not a conversation I want to have again."

"I feel you, man. I get it. I understand, believe me. I didn't want to say anything when the other two were here, because they'd want in on this, and I don't think they're ready for it. Not like you. I've seen other people come away from this saying they've been reborn, but I don't think Chris or Brandon would appreciate it the way you would, man." He lowered his head and made the face that told Lance a 'but' was forthcoming. "But it's not exactly legal. And we're not talking Golden Gate illegal. It's a bit more… underground than that."

It wasn't like he'd never been arrested. Hell, he did it on purpose twice for the views on his YouTube channel. Nah. It wasn't fear that made him curious and apprehensive; it was how quiet Collin was being. He never held anything back from Chris and Brandon. Where one of them went, they all went. But who were these other people he talked about? "What is it?"

"It's about as extreme as you can get, man. You're always talking about chasing the dragon. Well, this is the dragon."

"Okay." Impatience with Collin's mystery tugged at his tongue. "What will I be doing?"

"If all of this" — Collin waved his arms — "everything we do for fun can be distilled down to us staring death in the face and knowing we can get away with it, that we can survive, yet there is that tiny possibility that something happens and we don't, then what do you need to do? What is that next step?"

"To lean in more. To get as close to death as possible and spit in its face."

"Nah, man." Collin looked around before edging closer. The bar lights twinkled like purple stars in his pupils. "Lance, you need to die."

2

Before sunrise the next morning, Lance walked the waitress to the door and kissed her goodbye, with no intention of ever calling her again. The sex started out vanilla, then picked up to something more exciting. When he slipped the condom off without her noticing, it gave him a bit of that rush he searched for. Yet, somehow, she noticed and said, "It's alright. You can fill me up, baby. It's so hot."

That ruined it for him. She wasn't supposed to like it; she was supposed to take it without saying a word. If she'd said something afterward, fine. It wouldn't have been a thing. But her knowing that he went in raw, wanting it, it just killed the whole vibe. He didn't want her permission; he needed her to not know. For a few minutes leading to a handful of glorious seconds, he had absolute control over what happened to her, to the inside of her body. Biological command. Yeah, he'd pay for the morning-after pill or an abortion, if she needed it. But that shit needed to stay where it belonged: after the fact, when she was on her way out the door.

He pulled out instead. Left her to wear it for a few minutes while he went to the bathroom and cleaned himself off. He tossed the used towel at her to wipe up the mess.

After grabbing himself a can of lime-flavored water, Lance sat down on the small futon in his studio apartment and stared into the neon purple sign shining in from the liquor store across the street. It was a constant in his life, that light. Odd, he thought. He railed against it for weeks after he first moved in. Threatening the landlord and the store owner who left it on after closing. Now, he doubted he could sleep without it. Not that he'd tried to sleep tonight; it was already nearly morning.

Lance wasn't so foolish to think that he was immortal. Death would get him the way it gets everyone. His father thought he was immortal, but death floated through the shadows, cornered him by the workbench in the garage where dad sat every evening after supper, downing vodka and unfiltered cigarettes. Death took him on his own turf, in the house he bought with the sweat off his back. This wasn't about cheating death. This was about conquering death in the only way he could: going into its world, making it face him, and letting death know it would only get him when he was ready to die.

He was in charge of his life. The master of his future.

Maybe he'd go sooner than later. Maybe not. It's not like he was the type to sit down and waste away like those overweight bookworms headed for their second heart attack. He moved, lifted, wandered. Lived. Movement drove him. He had to do anything but sit and daydream. 'Imagination' could stay with the losers and the lazy. Hell, he didn't even need a stable job; thousands of couch potatoes clicking through their phones drove enough ad revenue to his YouTube channel for him to afford an adventurous lifestyle.

He would go when he chose.

Lance walked over to his bed and pulled a crumpled piece of paper out of the pocket of his cargo shorts and smoothed it against the wall.

3rd Street Alley. 9PM. The Clinic. Look for the center of everything.

Collin's paranoia irked him a little. He'd made it sound as if someone would kill him if Lance let slip the location. That made little sense, since he said right after,

"The place moves every few days, and it's never in the same place twice in the same month. Whatever you do, don't get caught."

What a sissy.

The thought of it sparked something inside of him, and the nervous energy built in his legs and groin. This was something interesting enough to get the blood flowing again. Too bad he'd have to wait all day, stewing, mulling the mystery. No drugs. No bleeding. Nothing too physical. A spiritual journey, Collin called it.

Sure, buddy. Whatever you say.

If, after 18 hours of waiting, bouncing on his toes with anticipation, there wasn't a good enough payoff, Collin would have to worry about him.

3rd Street Alley didn't bring him to a clinic, it brought him to some suburban dumpster dotted with brick buildings, boarded up doors and windows, and the weirdest graffiti he'd ever seen, like some tagger with a sci-fi fetish went apeshit with the pink spray paint.

Stray dogs and cats darted between wild bushes and lawns so overgrown that weeds grew out of the cracks in the foundations and neglected sidewalks. The air stunk of wet concrete and burning tar. He wondered how many of the cars parked along the street were stolen and left to rust. None of them had license plates, and only a few had windows.

The eerie stillness picked at him. Sounds from the highway and the roar of jets overhead were pervasive in any place this close to the Twin Cities, but most places still had other noises. Kids screaming at each other, people laughing, music. Anything but this creepy silence.

The sky was getting darker, so Lance widened his stride and tried to outpace the sunset.

After a block, a large brick building with a peaked roof loomed ahead. Unkempt arborvitaes lined broken concrete stairs like green fingers reaching up from the ground. Stained glass windows so blackened with soot and grime that Lance mistook them for painted brick until he noticed a flash of violet light illuminating a corner for a second before it ducked away. Rusted iron railing led to a pair of steel doors that looked untouched by the elements, almost new.

He reached out for the handle, but a voice from his left made his stomach leap.

"You looking to get well?"

A short man in an oversized military surplus jacket, dirty shorts, and filthy toes sticking past the straps of crumbling flip-flops stepped up to Lance. Silver rings sat in a line on his eyebrows, several of them held stiff by puckered and flaking skin coated in a yellowed crust, and black rings stretched and widened his nostrils so much that Lance could see his sinuses. His voice was limp and shaky. "I got your hook up right here, son." The man regarded Lance with a faraway, clouded look, then added, "You look too healthy for this shit, friend. I mean, I've sold to athletes and shit, but you can tell who uses and who don't, and you don't, man. Do yourself a favor and fuck off." He turned away and plodded back to his spot between a tall bush and a stone planter filled with cigarette butts and weeds.

Lance knew 'getting well' was slang for heroin use, and Collin promised him there would be no illegal drugs involved in this. Maybe he had the wrong place. He should probably get the hell out.

But he'd been waiting all day. All day. Nah. He wasn't about to leave.

"This isn't the Clinic?" he asked.

The man coughed a laugh. "Man, you ain't never seen a church before?" He waved a dismissive hand. "Beat feet, Narc. Ain't nothing here for you."

Being on the wrong side of town at night didn't faze him as much as the possibility of getting to the Clinic late and missing out on whatever waited. "Like being reborn," Collin had said.

Lance wasn't about to let some nasty, half-passed out junkie chase him away. "Tell me where the clinic is," he demanded. When the guy didn't flinch or open his eyes, Lance barked, "I'm looking for the center of everything. If it's not here, where the hell is it?"

The junkie's eyes opened with more clarity than Lance expected, and when he jumped to his feet with a sober nimbleness, Lance took a defensive step backward. "Ah, that Clinic." The man smiled with a mouthful of teeth blackened with rot but still dotted in places with white, as if he held the fetid night sky between his gums. "My mistake." Without looking away from Lance, he pounded twice against the door, paused, then pounded again.

The door creaked open, releasing the muted hum of music into the world.

"The doctor is in, friend." He indicated the entrance.

Lance hesitated. It was pitch black inside.

The junkie pointed upward at the contraption of bicycle chain and small hydraulic pistons. "It closes in ten seconds, and it won't open for you again. Shit or get off the pot, man. Ain't nobody in there that can hurt you. Just be cool and keep to the right."

3

Lance gave a look to the handful of stars peeking out behind the growing cloak of night slashing across the sky, then walked inside and counted the ten seconds it took for the machine above to whir to life and shut the door at his heels, bathing him in darkness.

He stared, waiting for his eyes to adjust. They didn't. His right hand pressed against the rough wall — so he didn't hurt his palm or damage the fingers that pulled his ripcord and used his diving regulator — he took tentative steps forward in the direction he thought he needed to go. Thoughts of invisible hands raking nails across his face, tearing at his sandy blond hair, or ripping out his throat intruded. His heartbeat raced.

Why didn't he bring a knife?

A click and a steady static hiss filled the darkness. Based on how the sound rolled around him, it seemed as if he stood in a narrow corridor.

"Wait there, please." A woman's high-pitched, nasally voice buzzed out of an old school intercom. He paused and waited like she asked. As he did, a dot of red light appeared on the wall like a tiny eye opening. "Look forward for me? A little higher. Right there, sweetness." She slurred as if she had something in her mouth. "Hold still."

He did.

A flash of blinding bluish white light pulsed from the wall ahead, and Lance slapped his hands over his eyes. More light, softer, filled the room as the sudden blindness faded. A petite figure backlit by a neon lavender glow stood in the doorway and reached out for his hand. "This way, hun. There you go. There's a step here, so be careful. Good job!"

Lance followed her inside.

The space opened. Wooden beams ran across the room, making an immense square underneath a vaulted ceiling that folded inward to form a sort of spike at its peak. Soundproof foam tiles covered the inside of the boarded-up windows. A thin haze of smoke swirled upward by large fans. A spider's web of wires hovered above, leading to purple spotlights and white stand lights illuminating a network of chairs and makeshift beds where the buzzing of tattoo guns and thudding of music mixed to make a beehive within a drum set.

Men and women covered in tattoos and with faces filled with shining hunks of metal curled up on trash futons and chairs while they sucked on their vape pens, passed around bottles of amber liquid, and chatted. If any of them gave a shit that he walked in, they hid it.

The wispy woman in front of him wore her hair in a pixie cut, parted down the middle, one half white and the other black. The strangeness continued downward, and he needed to squint to see her clearly. On the left side of her face, her eyebrow was a steel caterpillar of concentric circles, each one progressively smaller than the next. An elaborate wing of eyeshadow curled upward, and her nose had a small diamond stud in it. The corner of her mouth upturned into a forced grin. On her right side — the white side — tattoos of stars that curled down from her shaved eyebrow, looped around a droopy eye, and settled into tears along her cheekbone and down to the corner of her heavily lipsticked mouth which was surgically altered into a frown. "You okay now, sugar?"

He understood why her voice slurred the way it

did. When she spoke, the two sides of her mouth competed against each other. She looked like the opposite halves of two angels. A pair of theater masks melded together.

Unease rumbled in his stomach. Why would a conventionally stunning woman do this to herself?

"Fine," he said. He took in the odd sights. He'd never been one for tattoos or piercings. That sort of lifestyle seemed strange to him. Too permanent. Too likely to get caught on something and ripped out. At least they looked sanitary here. The whole place practically stank of mildew, latex, and alcohol. He doubted the ambient air would pass a breathalyzer test. "I don't think I'm in the right place."

"Sure you are." She cocked the happy side of her head and smiled. Even her dress parted down the center; stripes on one side, squares on the other. "Seymour wouldn't have let you in if you weren't." She offered him a hand filled with rings and painted fingernails. "I'm Thalia. This is the Clinic."

He gave her dainty hand a squeeze, careful not to crush her fingers between all that metal. "Thalia. Seymour? I could smell why you keep him outside."

Thalia's frown side deepened. "He does that when he's on door duty. It keeps most of the curious folks away. He's really a sweet guy once you get to know him. He's really brilliant, too. Has his master's degree in mathematics." She spun on the toes of her boots and said, "Follow me."

She led him through a maze of progressively stranger procedures. A woman was having the whites of her eyes tattooed pink next to a bearded man getting a half-moon and three stars branded on the top of his foot. Lance had to turn away from the blackened raw flesh, as well as the mouthwatering smell of seared pork rising from it.

A table over, someone's front teeth were being filed to points.

A steel, cage-like construction took up the center of the floor. The six segmented legs covered up their lengths with bolts looked more like metal tentacles than the foundation for a hoist from which a heavily tattooed man hung suspended by thin chains connected to shining hooks that pulled and stretched triangles of skin upward. Lance's stomach dropped to his heels when he saw how the fattest hook in the center pierced through the bottom of the man's chin and out of his mouth.

"Keep up, sugar." Thalia giggled. "Everyone looks like that their first time."

His voice tightened an octave higher. "Like what?"

"All eyes, jaw open, color drained from your face.

Don't worry, you're still handsome. I'm sure it'll take more than a few needles to freak you out." She looked over her shoulder with her smiling side. "Do you have a girlfriend, Lance?"

He had to widen his stride to keep up with her quick, little steps. "I, uh, I d-don't."

"That's a shame." She winked.

Next to a person of indeterminable gender having chunks of their ear cartilage removed with a scalpel was a woman whose face was a pierced and tattooed mask of euphoria. Her blouse hung open, revealing slight breasts with pierced nipples separated from the center of her chest by blue towels taped to her skin. A hole in the center of the towel made room for the artist to slice away a heart-shaped hunk of skin, exposing the bone.

"I'm giving her my heart," the woman said, listlessly.

Her partner lifted their surgical mask and kissed her.

"It's impolite to stare, Lance." Thalia looked over her shoulder and grabbed his hand, pulling him along.

He did his best to not stare, look, or make eye contact, but short of closing his eyes, he couldn't help himself. And when they reached the area with the white curtains soaked in purple light, Lance found his feet riveted to the floor. Through the part between the sheets, he saw a thin man covered in ink, his feet in stirrups. A woman held his hand as a bald person wearing a black facemask slid a scalpel up the entire length of the bottom of his penis, opening his urethra like a tiny, fleshy book.

Dizziness overtook him. He couldn't look away.

Thalia turned around, placed her hand on his hip, and pushed him off to the side. Her frown side regarded him with sympathy. "Hey now. Listen — this isn't for you, okay? This is what these people came for. Judging by the looks of you, this isn't what you came here for. Is it?"

Lance shook his head. "No," he managed from his tightening throat.

"Nothing like this is going to happen to you. Not unless you want it. Even so, there's a waiting list and conversations that need to be had first." She nodded to the dozen and a half toolboxes and curtained areas. "Some of these people have waited over a year for this. Like you, they're all searching for something greater, something that transcends the simple definitions of self and identity. Their journeys brought them here. This is their next step in becoming one with something more."

"I can't imagine how they'd find anything through this." Lance swallowed. "It's morbid. Disgusting."

"This isn't that different from anything you've probably done," Thalia admonished. "People who are quick to shun us are often those with no problem scarring themselves internally. Drugs, alcohol. There are men who train for years to inflict violence on other men. Families bring their children to churches in order to put the fear of God into their heads, and they do it over and over. Folks jump out of airplanes for the thrill of fear, leaving an indelible mark on their psyches — a scar — that after the first time becomes a memory they chase and chase until they find something else to fulfill that desire, another extreme this or that to give them that rush that rips away the scar tissue over their memory. The only difference between them and us is that we wear our scars and our memories on the outside." Her head cocked over to her happy side, and her smile widened too far, almost to her ear. "Believe it or not, Lance, everything you're seeing here is an act of love. Self-love, to be sure. But I would argue that the only greater love is a mother's love. D'you know what I mean?"

His mother died when he was eight, and he didn't enjoy thinking about her smile or how her skin glittered with gold dust and smelled like the wind blowing fresh seawater inland on a cloudy morning. He hated her for leaving him alone with the stink of stale beer and the buckle end of a belt.

Thalia's sad side flipped upward at him. "Come on,

sweets. Your journey has brought you here to the center of everything. And she's this way."

Lance plodded along, mind caught between neon pink reality and waiting for Collin to jump out with a video camera and a group of his friends and laugh at the elaborate prank they pulled on him. Instead, he found himself conducted down a dark hallway with a single door at the end. An ominous white line glowed underneath it.

A twinge of fear twisted near his navel.

A hunched figure stepped out of the darkness to greet them. "Thalia? Is he going in? Can I go, too?" The strobing light behind them illuminated his face from orchid, to violet, to pink. He had round implants under the skin of his forehead in the shape of the Big Dipper, each one tattooed with a purple star, and his ears looked elongated. Not pointed like the elves in those movies, but stretched out and curved, as if someone added more cartilage to the backs of them to make them stick out more. He alternated rubbing his hands together over the pocket of his hooded sweatshirt and slicking back his glossy hair as he approached Lance. "Please? I won't say anything to anyone, I promise."

Thalia stepped between them. Her tone was sharp, yet caring. "Frankie, you know what she said. You went in there once already. You can't go back again."

"I know, I know! But I didn't mean it." Frankie's face bottom lip trembled, and tears thickened against the steel bar through his tongue. "She doesn't talk to me anymore. I-I-I can't hear her. I can't hear her!" Frankie's enraged voice echoed over the music and the buzzing.

Gently, Thalia rested her palm on his chest. "Frankie, you know what she said, so tell me what she said."

"I don't wanna." He bit down on his thumb with a childlike groan.

"Frankie?"

He squeezed his eyes closed and balled his fists. For a moment, Lance thought he might punch Thalia, but her soothing voice settled him down. "She said I can't go past the door anymore."

"But you can sit outside." She patted his shoulder. "It's okay, Frankie. It's okay. She won't stay mad forever."

"But I can't hear her."

"I know! But it's okay." She folded him into her arms. Her head only came up to his chest, yet he hunched down to rest his ear on her shoulder. "Where's your bear, Frankie?"

He pointed to the door behind him.

"Go get it and sit right here. I'm going to say goodbye to Lance, and you and I can sit here together, okay?"

"Okay."

Thalia patted him on the head and faced Lance. Her petal soft voice dripped with sympathy and care. "Frankie's had a rough life. Not everything turns out the way we want, right?"

Lance could only nod.

"This is where I leave you, handsome. The doctor is through the door. You don't even have to knock; just go straight in and close it behind you. She'll take care of everything else." Her happy side cupped his jaw with tenderness. "You made the right choice."

The thudding of his heart and Frankie's sniffling made it hard to distinguish what she said. It sounded like 'you're the right choice.' Clearly, that made no sense.

Thalia guided him forward a couple of steps before letting him go on his own. He looked back, unsure and nervous. It was an odd sensation made all the stranger by the hum of noise and the pulsating amethyst lights.

Get a hold of yourself, he told himself. All he saw was a bunch of weird body modders doing shit that was probably borderline illegal. His temple was clean. Untouched. If any cops raided the place, they'd see he obviously stood out amid this crowd. And it wasn't like any of them were in a condition to stop him if he had to run or fight his way out. Thalia said the doctor behind the door was a woman, so he wasn't trapped with someone strong enough to stop him from leaving. And if he had to charm his way out, he could do that, too.

His legs stiffened as he turned away from Thalia and Frankie, and with heavy feet, Lance walked over and opened the door.

4

Clinical light and the burning reek of bleach bathed the room. A cold, stainless steel dissection table with a thin foam pad and a small pillow on top waited in the center of the floor. Various monitors and machines sat heaped inside stolen shopping carts. A narrow counter with a tiny sink held a row of perfectly arranged syringes and vials sitting on a green towel.

There was a very Frankenstein vibe to the entire room, except for the smoking hot woman reclining in an office chair, her bare legs sticking out of the split in her lab coat.

She was exotic. Half black or Puerto Rican or something. Waves of black, shoulder-length hair settled shone in the light, streaking from her scalp to the large hoop earrings dangling from her ears. Under the opening of her lab coat, blue and black tattoos followed the arch of her collarbone and the curve of her breasts. When she stood up, her stiletto heels clacked against the floor, and a black skirt slid down the visible part of her thigh. A brass nameplate with black lettering read: Dr. FunGirl.

Relief cascaded down his shoulders and past his calves, pressing his tension into the floor. Lance smiled to himself. Of course, Collin. Of course. Only you would do something this elaborate to get me a hooker, you dirty bastard.

The worry that built while being dragged through the sideshow shifted to a giddy fluttering in his stomach. It tickled, and he laughed, his confidence returning.

Wetting his lips and allowing his eyelids to relax and give him that 'dreamy look' so many women liked, he strolled into the center of the room with a non-committal smile. "Look, I know you—"

"Don't give me those 'fuck me' eyes," she snapped. "I'm not here for that." She aimed her scalding hot coffee glare at his face and stood tall, shoulders back. "Keep that little thing in your pants." A faint but noticeable distortion slid past some of her words. Maybe she was foreign?

Whatever. He had met women like this. Man haters who turned to BDSM to release their feminine rage. They were easier to handle than they thought — you just let them feel like they have the control. "Alright. Where do you want me?"

She jabbed her chin at the table.

He hopped onto the pad. The weight of his head crunched the paper pillowcase. "So, if you're not here to—"

"I'm not here for you to gawk at, dip stick. And I don't make chitty-chat with man whores. I have to move all of this shit in, set it all up, deal with your ass, then move this shit out. I'm tired. On top of that, we're trespassing, and what I do is insanely illegal. That means our clock is ticking. So shut up, lay back, and let me work." She shook her head and muttered something to herself.

She probably couldn't handle him, anyway.

Just lying there purposely motionless was uncomfortable. His bladder started filling, and his fingers and toes constantly wiggled their complaints. He managed to keep himself still and silent for the several minutes it took Dr. FunGirl to plug in cords, flip switches, and turn dials on all her weird machinery. His stomach fluttered when she picked up a long needle twisted it into a syringe.

"Collin said no drugs."

"These aren't drugs in the sense you're think-ing of. It's a two-part serum designed to lower your heart rate while maintaining a minimum level of oxygen in your brain."

"Are you serious?"

She flicked her bisected tongue at him. "Serious as syphilis."

Nervousness blossomed back into tension. "What's the deal here? I've been to some strange places and met some fucked up people, but this sort of shit is out of my element."

She spun on her toes, facing him while she filled a second syringe with a mint green fluid. "I'm going to kill you, Lance. I'm going to hook you up to some monitors, stick an IV in your hand, put some flashing lights in your face, inject you with this delicious stuff, and dim the lights in your brain until it's just about to turn off completely." She squirted an arc of fluid out of the needle. "You're go-ing to die, Lance."

He hopped up onto his elbows. "Whoa, wait now. I didn't —"

"Oh, don't worry, Chicken Little. It's only for a few seconds. The point isn't to make you die permanently; it's to keep you at the transition between life and death — that place with the tunnel and light and dead parents, and whatever else." Before he could say anything more, she shoved a silicone mask that reeked of chlorine over his nose and mouth. "Breathe. This will hyper-oxygenate your blood, so your brain doesn't run out of air, and you end up a vegetable."

"Kill me? Vegetable? Is this for real? What the hell is all of this?"

She blew an impatient huff out of her nose and slid a third, fatter needle back into its sanitary bag with a crinkle. "If you don't want to do this, get the hell out. I don't do refunds, and I don't do crybabies. I get paid to do weird shit that nobody else will do for you jack-off, thrill-seeking dudebros, and it's attracted some unwanted attention that I have to concern myself with while you're lying here talking yourself into finding the balls to do this."

"Hey, I'm not down with putting junk in my veins."

"This isn't heroin or meth or any other bullshit." She shot him a sharp look, causing her hair to slide angrily over her shoulder. He couldn't help but find her irritation incredibly sexy. "Full disclosure: while this shit isn't exactly FDA approved, it's not addictive. Your poor little temple of a body isn't going to crumble and turn you into some kind of drug-addled junkie. This is only going to readjust your narrow perception of life and reality by turning the dial of your mental clarity up to eleven."

When Lance didn't immediately respond, she leaned in close enough for the floral bouquet of her hair to sneak through the mask. Her smile was a thin, red slice across her face. "Listen, I don't have a ton of time to stay in one place for long, so either get on board with Dr. Fun-Girl and get ready for the greatest thrill of your life, or you hike up your skirt, strap up those Mary Jane's, and get the fuck out of my lab." She paused for it to sink in. "Last chance."

He was stunned. Nobody ever talked to him like that. Guys, maybe, when they were jacked up and peacocking — getting alpha on the adrenaline — but never a woman. Not like this.

Shit, she was almost intimidating.

A wave of doubt lingered its way up the inside of his thighs. Collin told him what this woman did was like drinking pure excitement. Sex in a syringe. He never tried it himself, but he said another guy told him it opened a door within him that made everything make sense. Sounded like hippie bullshit. A bad LSD trip. Lance wasn't sure about this.

"Lancey," she shook the IV needle at him, "do you want to take a rocket to heaven or not?"

Realization crested cold at his chest. When was the last time he felt this nervous, this alive? Where every muscle tingled with anticipation and a touch of apprehension? This was an opportunity to ride the rush like a surfboard to somewhere few people had ever gone. He just needed to get out of his own head and do it.

"Yeah. Screw it. Let's do this." Lance forced his head deeper into the pillow.

"Good boy."

Dr. FunGirl readjusted the mask on his face, tightened the elastic band around his head, and then moved around the room with automated efficiency, flipping, turning, dialing, and walking back to unbutton his flannel shirt. Round sensors were planted onto his chest, and his forehead sprouted wires that led to beeping machines with hot air whirring out of their vents. A plastic heart monitor pinched his index finger like a clothespin. The fat needle painlessly slid into the vein in the back of his hand. She kept it in place with a Big Bird bandage.

She showed him two syringes. "This" — a clear fluid — "is going to keep your heart beating."

"What's in it?"

"Don't worry about it." The next syringe was filled with a green solution. "This is going to make your brain slow wayyyyyyy down, effectively killing you for about a minute."

The lump in his throat froze a path to his stomach, where it exploded like fireworks and sent icy sparks racing through his veins. His breathing picked up.

This. This was exactly the sensation he was chasing.

"Cool. Fuck yeah. How do I wake up?"

"It wears off." A hand on his chest lowered him back to the pillow. Dr. FunGirl stuck the first needle into the port under the IV bag, then the second. She swung what looked like a projector in front of his face, flashing beams of yellow at slowly increasing levels of brightness. "Just follow the light home."

The flashing projector made a hypnotic click, click, click, and Lance began to feel warm and cottony and floaty. Cool air crawled up his nose and dried his mouth. He fought against sleep for what felt like minutes, then slowly gave up. The solution in his veins worked like a masseuse under his flesh, tiny hands kneading his muscles into a stiff goo. It was almost too good, too relaxing.

His eyelids fluttered, and the world went black.

5

It was a dream of floating, flying, of existing as the cool breeze at the corner of the evening sky with such crystalline clarity that he knew the difference between a cumulus and stratocumulus cloud by the how electric they tasted.

He changed, rolled inward, knees curled up to his chest, and became a raindrop falling at such an alarming speed that his stomach pinned to his spine and breathing became an imaginary action he only distantly remembered being able to perform. When he splashed down, he was a boy standing in front of his father, before he left Lance and his mother all alone. It was the day his father gave him his first blaze orange hunting jacket.

Lance's eyes followed the thick veins in his father's well-defined forearm up to biceps that stretched taut against the sleeves of a black t-shirt as he thrust Lance's favorite stuffed monkey out toward the darkness.

"He's only seven, Harold," his mother's voice complained from somewhere isolated and out of reach.

"He's a man, now. He's doing man things from now on."

A tearing and a popping of fabric. A stab in his stomach burned up his nose. Lance fixed his eyes on the world of orange in his hands and the doors it would open.

"Men don't cry, Lance." The last words his father said to him.

Gravity twisted its way around his ankles and up to his hips. It pulled him downward into the lavender scents of first girlfriends, smeared his skin with fresh earth, ground his bones against crunching rocks, and pinched his lungs through caramel clay until a cave of sparkling diamonds yawned before him — the heart of a planet-sized geode thrumming with such energy that his body constricted and contracted in a series of orgasms that rolled in waves from his toes to his eyes and echoed along the shimmering walls of the cavern within his own soul.

This, he thought. *This.*

Everything folded inward. His consciousness detached from his human form as he hurtled through a tunnel of shifting geometric patterns vibrating with neon blue and pink light and smelling of ozone. Forever and ever, it went on. Light after light, shape after shape, whizzed by until the blackness opened its arms to him.

He floated in the infinite. Planets, stars, and nebulae stretched out before him. There was no end. There was only the singularity, the ultimate. Everything connected to him, and he connected to everything. Nothing, no universe, no heaven or hell, could surpass this. This.

Then the woman appeared.

She was tall and thin. Damp curtains of long, dark hair hung heavy across the pale skin of her bare breasts. Streams of gas clouds shimmering with worlds waiting to be born writhed behind her like impossible tentacles. He felt her looking at him, but the details of her face were obscured to a blurry non-existence. It didn't matter. Even though he couldn't see all of her, he instinctively knew she was both someone he'd never met before and everyone he'd ever met.

She could be anything she wanted.

"Who are you?" His voice echoed, but there had been no sensation of air passing through his throat, no slight tickle of speech. Speech didn't exist here. It didn't need to. If he wanted to speak, he only needed to will it. "What is this place?"

She lifted her hand. Claw-like fingernails dripped with a dark substance that stained the puckered skin of her fingertips. In the center of her palm sat a pearl of pulsating rainbow light.

When she spoke, her voice was pain, needles dragging along eardrums until they popped hidden blisters within the roots of his teeth that spilled their acid down along the tender ribs of his windpipe.

"Take this and know."

Lance reached out and took the pearl, if only to make the agony stop.

Everything calmed. No wind, no pain. Just silence. Beautiful, unending silence.

And he knew. He understood everything.

The pearl in his fingers throbbed brighter and brighter and brighter, the beating heart of a star. Each beat brought a new clarity, a silken understanding opening the secrets in his mind like the petals of a lily in the morning sun.

He knew everything.

The secrets of the world, the depths of the cosmos, how each living and non-living creature was all connected — dust motes bouncing and vibrating upon the harp strings of the infinite. He knew it all. He knew everything! And he laughed, because he realized concepts like finite and infinite, chaos and order, life and death had no meaning — they weren't real! He knew it because even the glowing pearl in his hand, this most wonderful of objects in the universe, wasn't even real. It was simply a —

...and a matter of —

...that existed within —

Lance awoke to a scorching ray of incandescent light burning an atlas of veins past his eyelids into the back of his brain. He slapped at the light with feeble hands as his body and mind slowly returned to consciousness.

"Easy peasy there, Cover Girl. Let yourself wake up." Dr. FunGirl pulled off the oxygen mask and moved the light out of his eyes. She looked him up and down, appraising, stopping only to smile at the wet, sticky area spreading through the lap of his jeans. "Was it good for you?"

No. No! It was gone. The pearl, the woman — it was all gone. Whatever it was he understood was charging away like a rocket burning away into the atmosphere, and no matter how far he reached with his mind, he couldn't catch it and pull it back.

DON'T LEAVE!

He shot up and tore the wires off his chest and face. "Send me back. Send me back! I have to go back!"

"What the hell, dude?" Dr. FunGirl stumbled backward. Lance swung his legs off the bed and stomped after her.

"Send. Me. Back!"

He took one more step before a tug in his hand sent pain spiking up his arm. Lance tore the IV needle out with his teeth.

"There's no going back, man!" She stared, her terrified mascara widening into two black circles.

"You don't understand. I had something. Had everything. I knew everything!" He grabbed her narrow shoulders and drove her back hard against the counter. "Put me back so I can find it again."

She grimaced. "It's one and done. I can't do this twice!"

"Don't tell me that!" Desperation and rage growled past his teeth. His vision blurred and narrowed around the doctor's face. The white world of the room darkened into the red of a fresh scab. He kept asking and asking, but she didn't answer. She just ignored him. Ignored! Did she think that would stop him? Was she expecting him to just forget everything and walk away like he didn't just experience having his every eye opened to the reality behind reality? How could she do that? Why couldn't she just send him back? How dare she take this away from him?

Why aren't you answering me?

Something thin and sharp pierced his abdomen.

Darkness retreated. The doctor's eyes were huge and bloodshot, her lips dotted with purple from the pressure of his thumbs against her throat.

She collapsed to the floor when Lance spread his hands in shock.

A needle stuck out of his stomach. It went deep, maybe into an organ. So deep that when he pulled it out, it felt like it took a piece of his stomach with it. He steadied himself against the counter.

For a moment, a distant part of him wanted to reach down and comfort her. A vision of soft, little hands yearned to run their fingers through her hair, to ease her. He tried to apologize, but she swung wildly. Her scream was scratchy and broken, the sound of glass shattering against a kitchen wall heard from behind a closed bedroom door. When her fist hammered against the counter behind her, it tipped one vial onto the floor.

The green fluid. Next to the sink was the clear vial.

A chill made his muscles solid again. She was choking, so that meant she was alive. If she was an actual doctor, she could take care of herself, he decided.

Lance swiped up both vials in his fist and ran out the door without a second thought.

6

By the time he got home, he realized the serum was gone. Only a few drops settled at the bottom of the green vial, and the bottle with the clear fluid was practically dry.

There had to be a way back to her. To everything.

Balled up in a corner, naked, and in complete darkness except for the glow of the liquor store sign, Lance watched the room and waited for something to happen.

Ever since he ran home that night, he noticed tiny changes in his perception. Everything in his apartment — his garbage can, the desk, his bed — was an inch out of place, a scant distance farther away than normal. It wasn't only the things at home. Somehow, the entire world was bent, curved upward around his feet so everything and everyone was an extra touch past his outstretched fingers.

He measured everything. The distance between the Stop sign and the No Parking sign. His arm, from shoulder to fingertip. The width and depth of his refrigerator. He measured and compared his findings to everything he knew had documented specifications. The door, how far the fire hydrant was from the curb, the height of the new cars on the sales lot. He even measured his erect penis, since he still had months old text messages sent to more than one woman saved on his phone.

A drop of hot lead fell to the bottom of his stomach when he put away the third measuring tape he used to measure the other measuring tapes.

Why did he do that? Why send unrequested photographs of himself to women? He could be proud of himself and his physique without needing to be obscene. Was it desperation? Arrogance? Insecurity.

He shouldn't care about that sort of crap. Sex was a numbers game. Count all the women — or men — in every city between home and Texas, and at least one of them will be in love with you without even knowing your name. And even if you didn't look good, more than a hundred would fuck you. Hell, he'd gotten a nibble from more than one woman by sliding a photo of his cock and abs into her DMs. It was just a game.

One with real people and genuine feelings, though.

Squeezing his eyes to shut out the thoughts, he went back to measuring.

The night after, the air thickened around him. A heaviness, as if gravity, on a whim, extended itself, stretched upward from the core of the planet just enough to add more substance to the atmosphere. He could only measure this with the scales in his bathroom and the one in the kitchen he used to portion his food. Like the tape measures, the scales lied.

Sleep became another matter. After an anxious week of running around and measuring everything, Lance found he didn't need to sleep anymore. Couldn't sleep, even if he wanted. The buzzing under his skin wouldn't let him. It crawled along his muscles, skittered along nerves and tendons like a train of ants tunneling its way in or out of his body. No matter how hard he scratched, how bloody his fingernails, he couldn't quell the wormy writhing awakening every nerve under his skin. There could be no satisfaction.

He needed to go back. To find her. Dr. FunGirl needed to send him back.

Lance showered, dressed, smeared antibacterial ointment on his weeping scabs, and for the first time in a week, left his apartment.

***

The church stayed dressed in graffiti and sheets of plywood, but even from half a block away, Lance could tell it was a corpse. Only its shell remained.

Seymour didn't hide from him in the bushes, and a stick held the door open a crack. Inside, only the stench of alcohol, latex, and mildewed fabric greeted him instead of Thalia's twisted face. Using the flashlight on his phone, Lance shuffled past gloves covered in ink and balled up paper towels browned with old blood and the discarded shower curtains used as privacy, and he made his way to the back where Dr. FunGirl had her lab. It was empty except for the greasy, half-rotted stuffed bear on the floor. He picked it up.

Lance stood in the doorway. He stared at the empty room while scratching the back of his hand against the roughest corner of the brick wall, leaving behind a smear of wetness and whatever hope he had of finding Dr. FunGirl that day.

Beneath the itching, he trembled. All the way to his bones. Anger and desperation mingled into a bubbling stew in his lower intestines. Why did they move? It wasn't like they made enough noise for anyone to call the police. They split dicks and drew tattoos in an abandoned church for shit's sake. It wasn't a drug cartel. What reason could they have to move?

How long did he wait?

No, he thought. It wasn't a matter of him waiting too long. They did something to him. Put something in his mind and under his skin, then ran off before he came back for answers. Collin would pay for this.

Of course. Collin. He knew how they moved. He had the address to the church, so he had to know where they'd be again. No way Collin would hold out of him. He'd know, and he'd tell.

If not, Lance would make him.

The noise of the door hinges squeaking open sent a chill up his back. He pressed the flashlight against his chest and stepped into the office, hiding behind the wall just inside the door. Hearing slow, sliding steps coming his way, Lance shoved his phone into his pocket, pulled his folding knife, and opened the blade.

The footsteps neared. Shuffling and slapping, as if the person's shoes were too big. Worried breaths and a puppy-ish whine bounced off the brick.

A sharp sting below Lance's thumb startled him, and he dropped the bear. He expected to see a needle or an insect — a spider — biting him but found the tip of the knife dug under a scab from where he absently scratched with the blade. He knew he should focus on the person about to enter the room, but the way one side of the scab clung to his skin like a door as he lifted it with the blade captured him.

Slowly, he peeled it back to reveal the red layer beneath. Electric cold prickled the nerves up his shoulder and settled at the back of his neck.

For a moment, the itching stopped.

Footsteps slid to a stop right next to him. He froze for a moment, then leaped backward and pointed the knife at the center of Frankie's chest.

"It's you," Frankie said, awe and surprise evident on his freckled face. His clothes were clean, mismatched, and smelled like a secondhand store. Someone must've given him a bath.

Frankie hesitated before picking up the bear. "Y-you came back."

"So did you."

Frankie smiled and gave the bear a little wiggle. His face became serious. "You heard her, didn't you? You heard her, and that's why you came back."

Lance squeezed the knife handle. The itching started again. "That's right, Frankie. I came back because I heard her. Where is everyone?"

"I heard her once, too. They said she chose me. Wanted me to receive her message." Frankie paced in a circle. "They hooked me up. I laid down on the bed. The Doctor gave me a shot, and-and-and-and then the flashing." He flicked his fingers opened and closed in front of his face. "Did she give you the flashing?"

Lance nodded. "Yeah."

Frankie's eyes bunched at their corners, and he looked near tears. "I went to sleep, and I heard her. I heard her. I heard her." A tear rushed down the side of his nose. "I heard her, but I can't remember. I can't remember anything. You! What did she say to you?"

A quick thrust of the knife stopped Frankie. "I heard her, Frankie. She told me everything. Now I want you to tell me some things." Lance stepped forward, driving him back a few steps more. "Where is the Doctor?"

Frankie shrugged.

Lance stomped his foot the way he would to get a dog's attention. Appropriately, Frankie jumped. "Where is she? Where is everyone?"

"I don't know," Frankie shouted. "They don't take me with them. They leave me behind and get me when it's time." His bottom lip trembled. "They leave me because I forgot. Because she still speaks to me, and I can't hear her."

Frankie threw down his bear and unbuttoned his collared shirt and flung it open.

Lance nearly vomited.

Rows of severed ears hung from the skin on Frankie's chest. Black, white, brown. Color didn't seem to matter until Lance's eyes spied the gangrenous ones roughly sewn onto infected flesh, dribbling with pus. At least two were shriveled and blackened with rot.

Frankie wept. "I can't hear her. She speaks to me, but I can't hear her. I just want to hear her one more time."

Lance covered his mouth as a sudden waft of fetid flesh slid up his nostrils.

Frankie dropped to the floor, wailing and rocking on his knees with his disgusting bear clutched to his chest, screaming for his mother.

Without a second thought, Lance shut the door and jogged out of the building. Even though Frankie didn't follow, Lance sprinted down the road to put distance between himself and the sickening scene. What had they done to Frankie? Was that what they were going to do to him? Tie him down and sew body parts onto his body in some kind of fucked up cult ritual? Who does this shit?

He just wanted his mother.

Lance flinched at the intrusive thought and kept sprinting. Maybe they already did something to him. The itching, the way the world flexed and bent, the fullness of the air. Whatever they did, they needed to fix it and hook him back up. Send him back to her.

No. There was no fixing him. They were going to send him back. He'd go to Collin's place and get the address of their new location. The doctor was going to send him back, whether she liked it or not.

He wouldn't end up like Frankie. No way.

7

Collin didn't return the phone calls or texts Lance left him over three days. Collin knew something. Frankie told him, and he bailed. He ran.

Maybe he's hurt? What if he's in trouble and he needs help?

"Shut up," Lance barked at himself as he peeled another scab and flicked it into his bathtub with the others. This one was a trapdoor leading into a basement filled with strawberry jam. When the itching subsided, he breathed a quivering sigh of relief.

It'd gotten worse since the first scratch, and he still hadn't slept. Three weeks with no sleep.

Fuck it. He didn't need it. Wasn't even tired. Every

bite of food and every drop of water went to keeping his engine running, and it ran at 100% efficiency.

He still dreamed, though. Snippets of visions that appeared in the tunnel of black whenever he stopped moving, stopped picking. Curved threads of spinning magenta light pinwheeled through a hole of infinite darkness hanging in the air between him and the center of his apartment. They spoke to him. Sometimes they spoke in a scream, forcing him to cover his ears with his fists and cry — quietly, just in case someone else heard.

When the visions stopped, the invisible maggots wriggling under his skin woke up and demanded release. One by one, from his chest to his legs, he'd open the doors to let the little squiggles of light float upward, through his ceiling and walls, to a freedom only they knew.

Sometimes, though, when the darkness of midnight reached out to embrace him, they spoke in soft, familiar slurring, struggled to form coherent words, yet he didn't need to strain to hear them. He remembered them, instead. Their thin, alcohol-laced rasps.

"Don't be scared, Lancey. You're such a good boy. I love you. If momma doesn't wake up, be a good boy for your dad. He won't hurt you again, not when I'm gone. Because I'm going to watch you from the sky. I love you."

I will, mommy.

His phone chimed its little tune two or three times before he crawled over and picked it up. It was a text from Collin.

Dude, are you alright? What are these messages? LOL. Just got back to my place from New Zealand. HMU when you get a chance.

His place.

Lance nearly ran out his door without clothing but stopped himself. He needed to approach this cautiously. Maybe Collin had been in New Zealand, maybe he hadn't. Maybe he and Dr. FunGirl planned this whole thing. Shoved the worms under his skin and filled his head with visions.

He needed to get back to her.

Lance took a scalding hot shower, ignoring the ruddy chips of solidified clots floating around pinkish water and spinning down the drain, dressed, and left some time before 3AM.

He brought his knife.

Lance knocked twice, his usual rhythm, but the prickles of pain scratched the itching on his knuckles, so he kept rapping his knuckles on the painted steel, watching the blood splatters take the shape of a dozen thin, twisted limbs reaching out from the sky gray door.

The deadbolt cracked free, and the door whipped open. Collin, wearing his bathrobe and a squint of fury, rushed forward.

Lance took a step back, hands raised in defense.

Collin's eyes widened. "Lance? Holy shit, man. What happened to you?" He led Lance into his well-furnished one bedroom. Sandalwood and sage mixed with old weed smoke and something greasy and old; Collin probably had pizza for dinner and left the box out. The heavy glass ashtray on the dinner table held the brown remains of a joint. The living and dining rooms shared the same space, the oak table and matching entertainment center separated by a soft blue couch and the four-light chandelier Collin turned on and dimmed to a comfortable yellow glow.

Lance wrung his hands together to keep from itching. He slid his wrists inside the sleeves of his windbreaker. "This place is always nice, Col. It's really nice. Y-y-you just got back from New Zealand? Do anything cool?"

Collin pulled a wooden chair from under the table and placed it between them. Voice low and grave, he asked, "Lance, be real with me, bro. Are you alright?"

He really cares.

This time, Lance didn't hush the voice in his head

or ignore the spreading warmth reaching outward from his chest to Collin, the man who was the closest person to a brother he had.

"I'm in a bad way, Colly. I'm losing my mind, man. I've been seeing things. I can't stop the itching." Tears rushed down his face. A hollow bruise at the center of his being begged for consolation, so Lance opened his arms and stepped toward Collin. "I'm just glad my best friend is home."

"Don't touch me," Collin hissed and leaped away.

Lance let his arms fall to his sides. Collin didn't care. Not the way he thought he did. They weren't brothers.

But they could be. He could feel the love inside Collin, the brotherly tenderness of two child cousins holding each other at a loved one's funeral, trapped inside him, waiting to be born.

Collin just needed to be freed.

"Whatever you got, I don't want it." Collin held up his hands and stared, a disgusted sneer on his lips. "You don't need me; you need a doctor."

"Yes!" Lance exclaimed. "I need the Doctor. The one from the church."

Collin looked confused. "Isobel? Why the hell do

you need her? She's not a doctor, man. She's just a nurse with a fetish I met online last year."

"What?" Lance felt a fire in his stomach extinguish. "No. She's a doctor. She hooked me up to machines and injected me with a serum." A vortex of panic spun in his chest. "She sent me to space. I heard her. She gave me a message, Colly."

"Dude." Collin moved himself and the chair closer to the living room. "She's just some freaky chick who pays me to spout some sales pitch to drum up interest in her escort business. You were all mopey and bitchy. I just thought you needed to get laid, so I paid her to fuck your hips loose, man. Two grand for whatever you wanted and more."

"No." Lance shook his head. "No, you didn't. You're lying, Colly. Don't lie to me." He unzipped his jacket and tore open his shirt, revealing the crags and ridges of oozing scabs covering his midsection. "She did this to me!"

Horror stretched Collin's face into a silent scream. Finally, he breathed, "Get the fuck away from me, you herpes-covered fuck!"

Lance didn't want to talk to this Collin; he wanted the other Collin. The one beneath. That Collin would understand.

He rushed past the chair and grabbed his friend by the shoulders, earning him an awkwardly thrown fist to the side of his neck. It pushed him more than hit, but he still had to catch himself on the dining table. Lance spun and ducked as Collin's other fist left a trail of musky wind under his nose.

Lance lashed out with a strike of his own, slamming the edge of the heavy ash tray into Collin's temple.

Collin crumpled onto the floor. The small gash on the side of his head erupted blood across his cheek and nose in the same spiraling pattern as Lance's visions.

He knew how to free his friend.

Over and over, Lance bashed the ashtray against Collin's skull. Each hollow strike cracked the shell of his sun-tanned cage, freeing bits of Collin in the spray of gore and hair painting the walls with the shattered bars of his prison.

But when Collin was finally free, Lance didn't feel any euphoria. Nothing jubilant leaped from within. No guilt, no sense of relief, only profound sadness.

An old voice crawled out of Collin's head and lashed the tenderest parts of Lance's ears.

"Real men don't cry, Lance. Now shut the fuck up and pull up your pants, or you'll get something to cry about.”

A final crunch pressed the front of Collin's shell inward and spat the wicked voice onto the carpet in a glut of crimson pulp.

Greasy smudges on Collin's phone revealed the four numbers he used for his password. The combination wasn't difficult to figure out once Lance remembered Collin's birthday.

Scrolling through his emails, he found a thread from a name he recognized, though it wasn't the Doctor's.

Thalia's email contained a simple message and an address on the other side of the Cities. Another quiet suburb, this one near the river. They'd be there in two days.

Lance forwarded the email to himself, gave his brother a goodbye kiss on the cheek, and headed home to wait.

8

Lance parked next to a gas station dumpster and watched Thalia from his car. She wrapped her hair in black and white fluffy pigtails, matching the silk stockings she wore under a short, tiered skirt. She hurried back and forth from her minivan, grabbing box after box and hauling them into the small, abandoned strip mall along a quiet highway frontage road. Like the church, someone already boarded up the windows.

He didn't want to have to kill her, but he was going to.

Thalia took the last box out of her vehicle and slid the door closed. Lance left his car and stalked through the brush bordering the parking lot until he reached the side of the building with the most concealment from the door. There he waited for Thalia to return to her van. She'd have her back to him, and there was no way she could outrun him in those heels. Not that she looked athletic to begin with. The boxes were probably the heaviest things she carried, aside from whatever emotional baggage she hauled around. Nah. Thalia was one of those women who was thin, soft, and warm. Someone comfortable and comforting.

Someone who could hold him when he cried.

He squeezed his eyes closed. *Shut up, shut up. Shut the fuck up.*

Using the building anger at his brain's constant intrusion and at whatever the hell she did in there that kept her from coming outside and letting him grab her from behind and stuff her into the back of her van, Lance grit his teeth and charged to the door, intent on doing what he came here to do: get her to tell him where the doctor was, then kill her to keep her quiet about it.

Inside, the building's emptiness opened up before him like a gaping maw. Dusty light groaned in from the windows, illuminating a broken tile floor with a swept path that looked like a tongue. Bare stud walls with electrical wires snaking around them disappeared into the darkness at the back of the room. Chips of rust fell from the ceiling as the whole building waited for him to reach the center of the floor before it clamped down on him like a crocodile's jaws.

She was waiting.

She stood in the middle of the room, several feet away from the resin tables atop which she'd stacked the boxes, her hands folded in front of her like a twisted doll from the 1950s used to teach women conservative manners. "Even in the daytime, it's scary in here. Isn't it?" Anxiety softened the corners of her voice.

Lance paused for a moment, then continued forward. He couldn't let anything stop him. Not when he was this close. He scratched off a scab, alleviating the itch so he could focus. "It's just the dark." He'd gotten used to the dark. Diving in underwater caves, climbing around underground ones, hiding under the bed from his father's belt.

Shut up.

"The dark wouldn't be so bad if the light was a prettier color than white and gray. It's just so… severe. You know?"

He nodded. In this room, the light looked harsh. The same shattering white of morning that broke through his windows while he slept and tore at his eyelids.

Keeping his eyes on her, he stepped over to the table and checked the boxes. "These are empty."

She nodded. Even though the path to the door was clear, she didn't stand like she was going to make a dash for it. "The first time I saw you, I thought you looked like a gentleman. One of those guys who would hold a door for a lady or help her carry heavy boxes out of her van. I thought that maybe you'd come over sooner, instead of sitting in your car for so long. It must have been uncomfortable."

Lance's eyes narrowed. "You saw me?"

She nodded. "You don't go around the world looking the way I look without noticing when people stare, even when they're hiding. It's a feeling I get at this point. Right here." She pointed at her heart.

The bleary glow smearing along the dark hid her face behind a diffusion of light, and Lance tried to blink away whatever blurred his vision.

A fist of cold slammed into his stomach.

Don't.

I have to do this.

"I know what you came to do." She hid the shivering in her voice behind the practiced mask of bravery worn by a woman who had been hurt more than once in her life. "I don't suppose you'd make it quick for me? I know it might not look like it, but I don't much like pain or being afraid."

Lance looked down at the masses of dried blood on his fingers and remembered he'd left his knife in the car. Going back wasn't an option, not when she could jump in her van and speed away. He'd have to do this with his hands.

"I'll try," he answered.

Thalia stiffened but didn't resist. The only noise she made was a shivering breath through her nose when he slid his hands around her slender throat and pressed his thumbs against her windpipe. He could feel terror radiating off her, as if her aura was painted with electricity that spoke to him in whispers, and he hesitated. The smell of her — bourbon and roses — fell on him in waves of experience rather than scent.

"It's okay," she said, her voice feather soft and frightened. "It's okay."

The background shifted, and he stood at the doorway of a dimly lit bedroom, watching as she struggled under the weight of her own intoxication, sputtering chunks of puke and yellow fluid out of her nose and mouth. Her swollen tongue lolled past her lips as she choked. When she tried to roll onto her side and clear the sick so she could breathe, rough hands clamped around her shoulders and her down until her stomach bucked and her useless legs kicked against his father's weight. After a minute, she gave one more crackling breath, a quiver, then went still.

"Turn around, Lance," his father ordered, but it wasn't his father's voice.

The world spun sideways and slowly returned to the dusty vacant room. Thalia was still in his hands.

He stared into her teary eyes, felt her throat move under the pressure of his thumbs as she swallowed.

He let her go. If she was surprised, he couldn't tell.

His shoulders slumped and he trembled. A sob burst from his mouth. "Everything hurts."

Shut up. Men don't cry.

Thalia's little fingers settled on his arm, and she gave it a reassuring squeeze. "She can make it better. For you, for me, for Isobel and Frankie. For all of us, Lance." Thalia took his hand and kissed his knuckles. She pushed up his chin with a ringed finger. "Can you hear Her?"

Lance wasn't sure. He wasn't sure he knew how to listen to her if she spoke to him again. But he saw things, felt things. Things not himself. Things from beyond his understanding.

"Yes," he said.

Thalia's smile side and frown side moved in tandem, giving him a sad smile. "I do too. She told me you were going to come here. Said that you would come here to hurt me, but that if you didn't, I could give you these."

She produced two vials from the pocket of her skirt — one clear, one green.

Gently, he took them out of her hand.

Thalia leaned closer and kissed his bottom lip. "The rest of your journey has to be on your own. I can lead you to the door, hun, but I can't go in with you."

Lance stared down at the vials while his mind raced and planned. He finally had them. He just needed a few more things, and he could go back to her. There was an end to this. A light at the end of this fucking tunnel, and he nearly had it in sight.

An involuntary laugh screeched from his throat, and he turned and ran, leaving Thalia with her boxes.

"Remember, Lance," her sweet, downy voice echoed after him, "everything we do here is an act of love."

9

It took Lance three days to find clean needles. He spent part of an afternoon waiting for the old man with the oxygen tank and mask to hobble far enough away from the crowded park so he could wrestle everything away without getting caught. That was the last thing he needed.

Please don't let that old man die.

Lance spent his morning focused on setting up the area around his bed and doing breathing exercises — deep in, deep out — to oxygenate his blood the way he did before a free dive. He could hold his breath for four minutes. Every half hour, he shoved a liter of water down his throat, which is how he would make up for the lack of an IV. He watched medical training videos and practiced sliding a needle into an orange, so he'd hit his vein. When he was confident enough he could do it, he wiped the needle clean of fruit oil and filled both syringes, not bothering with exact measurements. He saw how much she put in them. Right up to the black line.

Maybe a little more, just to be sure.

He could do this. It was easy. Too easy. No problem. In and out. He only had to make it a minute.

Ex-girlfriends would laugh at that.

He laughed at that.

The butterflies in his stomach were frightened away by the crazed hornets of exhilaration. This. This. He kept it repeating aloud and in his head. This was it. This was the peak. After it, none of this shit would matter. He could fly on his own. Travel to planets. Breathe dirt. Feel… lights in his skin. Something. If he could remember what it was, he wouldn't have to do this shit.

Breathe.

Lance lay in the middle of his bed, started a 10-hour video of a flashing screen on his laptop, and tied a bungee cord around his arm, crushing scabs and sending delightfully sharp stings of pain ringing through his blood.

First, the clear syringe. Then the green.

He unwrapped the cord, started the oxygen, laid back, and set the laptop on his chest just as three hard knocks hit his door.

GO AWAY!

This would only take a minute. Just a minute.

This time, the darkness took him swimming through a mountain.

He tasted snow and breathed copper. Everything moved for him, invited him, whirled around him like the time he filled the sink with water and pulled the plug just so he could stick his little fingers in the center of the little tornado that formed in the drain.

He was the tornado. He was its center. The center of everything.

Down and down he went, jetting through crust and mantle, flying through rainbows of galaxies, and folding himself inward until he became the center of a distant sun going supernova. He exploded again and again and again until there was nothing but ecstasy, the pure and burning rapture of being alive and staring through the darkest shadows of death.

She was there, wrapped in a gossamer cloud of shimmering midnight and in a place that only existed when the whipping berry and magenta lights behind her touched it. Her hair slithered around her like a meadow of snakes standing on their tails.

In her outstretched palm, she held the pearl for him.

Lance reached his fingers out, flinching internally at the expectation of the shock of misery brought by her voice. But she remained silent.

He took the pearl.

She placed a finger to lips that both existed and didn't. "Shhh," was the sound of a jackhammer in slow motion.

His brain rattled and bounced around his head, a pinball slamming against yellow and green and white lights. Black then green, black then yellow. It wouldn't last, though. It wouldn't. Even if it did, he had it. It was his. Clutched in his fist was the pearl, and it was his. And he knew. Beyond the incessant pounding and the growing pain, he knew.

He knew and floated.

He knew and flew.

He knew and burst open into stars.

"Welfare check!" a man's voice called out.

A woman's voice was next. "Police department! Hello?"

Lance ignored them as he awoke, reluctant to give up the sensation of floating, the numbness, the knowing. He knew, though. Still knew. He didn't have to give it up.

"Lance? Hello?"

They were already in his apartment. He'd likely have to meet them and explain what it was he was doing, if they could even fathom even a fraction of the infinite that churned within the dark brilliance in his mind.

Nah. He would just make them go away.

Expectation turned to confusion and worry when he tried to lift the laptop off his chest and his arms didn't respond.

It's okay. I'm just waking up.

He could still see, could feel. The steady rise and fall of the laptop on his chest told him he was breathing. Air flowed against the hairs in his nose, filled his throat, but the rest of his body was an unspoken word.

And the itching. The incessant itching of a thousand centipedes crawling and squirming around every inch of skin, tickling every hair, rooting around his every pore with the tips of their needle legs.

Just one scab. Just one. He had to open a door and let them out.

No matter how hard he struggled, he couldn't move. Come on. Move. He tried to sit up, but there were only faint butterfly wing tingles in the crooks of his elbows and the bends of his fingers. *Please, please, please. Don't let this be happening.*

Terror dribbled a stream of moisture down the corner of his right eye. It pooled in his ear.

Everything was split. His mind and body disconnected from each other. He had no control. Couldn't hold his breath, blink, move his tongue, or even staunch the stream of warm piss pooling between his legs. Fear raged in his mind while his heart beat evenly and his body stayed calm, teasing him with the ideas of movement, the legend of mobility.

No, no, no.

There had to be something. Anything. Happiness, sadness, fear — anything that would make his body respond and assure him this was only temporary, that it would be over fast, wear off in a minute. But no matter how hard he tried, his heart rate wouldn't pick up. There was no fluttering in his stomach. No constriction in his rectum. His teeth vibrated and his jaw groaned on its hinges but there was nothing to tell him he was alive, to reassure him that this was just falling or drowning or anything that said he was alive — *God, just please let me panic! At least let me panic!*

"Hello!" the woman yelled.

I'm here! Over here!

"Oh, shit."

His icy toes warmed at her touch as she shook his foot. For a moment, he thought he would gasp in surprise, tense in elation, but his body stayed limp, his pulse even and indifferent.

She shined a penlight into his eyes and urged, "He's alive. Radio the paramedics. Get the Naloxone."

"I don't think this is heroin," the male officer said.

"I don't care what it is. He's OD'ing on something!"

Though he couldn't move, he felt everything, every touch. A sheet of stiff linen tickled his leg hair as they jostled him around, plopped him onto a gurney, and wheeled him out of the room into the dank diesel and concrete air where he was shelved into the awaiting ambulance. Saliva pooled in the back of his throat as they drove, leaving a maddening tickle he couldn't cough away, couldn't choke free, couldn't gag while it slithered down his throat like an earthworm.

Yes! Please let me drown. I can't live like this. Please! No.

No!

A thin tube crawled between his cheek and the oxygen mask, sucking out the spit with a feathery tickle of air against his uvula.

Every sensation amplified, making the new ones that much more unbearable. Sliding the tube up his nose and down his throat into his lungs. The sharp agony of the catheter being force fed down the sensitive tip of his penis and the swelling of its balloon in his bladder. A thick needle jabbed into his hand. The heart monitor pinched onto his finger. Through it all, he couldn't scream, couldn't beg. His only comfort was he had people around him. People were there to save him, to help him.

Please. I'll give you anything. Dad? Mommy!

When they took away his sight with the damp mask, there was no fading to sleep in the black. No happy visions to ease nerves that burned to move. No faceless woman. No pearl. No sweet dreams of flying or swimming or fucking, just darkness. He couldn't dream. Couldn't, but he needed it. The very center of his soul screamed to dream, to paint stars and nebula against the black. He was always so close, but each time the tantalizing neon flash of an image blinked into his mind, it retreated into the endless abyss of non-existence, the incessant beeping of a heart monitor, the huff and whoosh of the ventilator, and the desperate shrieks of his own voice caged within the emptiness of his own mind.

10

They moved him. He couldn't see who it was, but he recognized her voice. Isobel — Dr. FunGirl — spoke with authority to the physicians in the room.

These are the papers that prove his identity. These show we are his next of kin. Yes, we understand the medical implications involved with leaving him in this state, and the private facility we are moving him to is more than equipped for handling his long-term care.

There was an argument. Men explained hospital processes and procedures to her in confusing words while they spoke in circles. Lance felt her impatience slice through the air and dig its spikes into the pulpiest spots of his soul, and he wanted to scream.

Once the word 'compensated' was uttered, another male voice stifled the others' arguments.

Not long afterward, hands strapped and unplugged, poked and moved. Rows of lights flashed hypnotically past as they wheeled him into the back of a large vehicle and brought him to his new home, a clean room with a commanding view of the blue sky and popcorn clouds and left him to scream inside his own mind.

One morning, Dr. FunGirl started the contraption under the bed that raised him into a sharper recline and wheeled him over to the window. From the colors of the leaves in the distance, autumn wasn't far away.

She dragged a chair next to him, sat, and held his hand. "I'm sorry, Lance. It has to be frustrating to have felt like everything is a matter of choice, living life as one decision to the next, only to discover that no matter what choices you could have made would have led you to any other outcome than being right here, right now. There were times when I felt like an inevitability, too. When I was someone else's foregone conclusion." She passed her thumb over a dry patch of healing skin. "It makes you feel smaller. Lesser than. Like your proper place is hiding in a corner, waiting to be summoned by people around you who command their lives and yours.

"But this isn't about control. I hope you understand that. This is about love.

"She chose you, Lance. Chose you as a vessel for Her final message to us. She's called others to us, to be sure. Frankie sacrificed his sanity to bring us here, to Minnesota, to you. Collin traded himself just so we could hear her again for the brief, beautiful second it took Her to speak your name. Before he hid for those few weeks after you found us, he told me that he knew you'd kill him, that he was meant to let you end him. But it didn't matter to him. He loved you. He called you his brother. And he was so happy that it was you She chose. He'd tell me, 'Lance is strong. Fearless. There's nothing he can't handle. And when the time comes, his voice will be the loudest.' He looked up to you. And it was his love for you that gave him the strength to face his fear of death and sacrifice himself. He knew that he could get you to do it. To free him. That's what he wanted most, for you to be the one to unlock his shackles. Now that he's free, the pain in his soul is quieted against Mother's breast.

"There's a process to everything, Lance. The changing of seasons. Births. Deaths. A process of letting go. As much as we love Her, we have to sacrifice to hear Her or be near Her. It's Her demand, and our privilege to, when called upon, proudly give our offering of flesh to Her.

"She comes from a time before time, Lance. Carried in Her womb stars that have long since burned out and spread to the outer edges of the universe like dandelions. Compared to Her, these silly, man-made gods are nothing more than mewling, confused kittens raging at the world while struggling to climb out of their cardboard boxes. She's everything. The greatest of great old ones. The true mother of us all.

"Her love and understanding calls to us, shows us how to transcend our physical forms to become one with Her, but we've become so blocked, so conditioned to forget, that we beat any true memories of Her out of our heads through distractions like television, religion, politics, and obsessions with our physical appearance. Those of us who believe, her children, we give little pieces of ourselves to Her to prove we haven't forgotten, haven't turned away, and that we will listen to Her voice — we still hear Her.

"Everything is an act of love. Every sacrifice lights the way for Her to come and make things right again. Oh, Lance, if you only knew how we all feel. More than anything, we want Her to come home and sing the truth to us — the lullaby that awakens us to eternity and returns us to lucidity. We do this for love. For love, and because we miss Her.

"I really wish you could want to be a part of this, Lance. I wish you could say you wanted this as badly as you wanted to hear Her again." She stoked the back of his hand. "Maybe you do. Maybe you do."

A long beeping noise summoned her to a place at the far end of the room, and she left him blanketed in the pleasant gleam of the sunshine for a moment before sitting back down.

"Understand that our human forms limit us. Whether we know it or not, we fear Her as humans fear things they don't understand. Sometimes too much. Yet, to those of us who could hear, She told us She would send someone — you, Lance — someone who wouldn't be as afraid as the rest of us. Someone more worthy than others of hearing Her, of calling to Her. This is why we've kept you alive these months. You're special, Lance. Mother wants to see you, to see the brightness within you. She said Her final message was within you, and that you would understand once you've transcended. Once your physical limitations have been removed."

She stood and, after kissing him on his cheek, said, "This will be over soon, Lance. I promise."

Autumn's pall had fallen over the city when Lance finally understood.

Time had no meaning anymore. All that had existed for spans of days and nights were his unsteady thoughts and the ever-present burrowing under his skin like beetles beneath the bark of an ash tree. The window they had him propped in front of reflected the him he would soon leave behind. A body once rippling with lithe and powerful muscle was now soft and thin. Every day someone came in to wash him with fresh rose water, running soft cloths over puckered scars, pink in their infancy. Sometimes, they would sing to him. Thalia liked to read him poetry while caressing him. Often leaving little kisses on his fingers and reminding him he was brave and loved. At first, he fought it. Struggled against the helplessness trapping him inside his body, keeping him immobile while wave after wave of tickles and crawling chilled him to the bone.

Then a sensation of feathery lightness lifted the cap over his mind, and it opened him.

He understood.

His body, his skin, was a cocoon for a great becoming.

The day had come.

A fluffy blanket of purple, blue, and gray clouds lingered over morning when people unhooked him from machines and tubes, and then transferred him to the bed that brought him up the elevator and into the chilly wind blowing over the roof where a group waited. Seymour, Frankie with his bear, Thalia, and several others he recognized by their piercings and tattoos. The woman with the heart-shaped scar on her chest. The suspended man. They smiled and touched his skin as they moved him to the center of the roof, strapped his lower half to the gurney, and lifted him into a standing position.

"It's time." Isobel wheeled a table filled with knives, scalpels, and razor blades next to him. The crowd came in closer. Latex gloves and long aprons were passed around and donned. "It's time for her to come back to us, Lance. Her babies need her." She chose a blade shimmering with the muted white glow from the clouds as a bar was lowered in front of him and his body leaned forward.

Isobel poked the tip of the blade into the flesh between his kidneys. With a voice thick with emotion, she whispered, "Cry for Mother, Lance. Bring Her home to us."

The blade coursed upward along his spine, and his blood wailed a song of sweet suffering. Others reached inside the flaps of his flesh to lift and pull the door open. Every agonizing inch, every squelching rip and tug of skin being peeled away from fat and muscle, liberated his light and sent his brightness into the sky, past the seen and unseen, reached through time. He was a star being born, a heavenly body freed from its cage, and the knife was the spark that lit the flame of his radiance that screamed, *Come home!* until he became a beacon for Her to find Her way to Her children.

For Mother.

Another cold bite of a blade slid through dermis, epidermis, and hypodermis. Clamps squeezed the corner of his flesh and jerked downward while sticky fingers rolled his human barrier from thigh to foot like a bloody stocking until toenails popped away with ten satisfying little clicks.

Isobel stripped his backside clean and carefully took his penis and testicles before working up his chest and around to the back of his back, preparing to pop him clean from his shell. With each freeing slice, Lance remembered. The pearl. Mother's voice, a sound he ignorantly thought hurt him. If he would've just listened, he would have known it was Her pain, Her agony at being separated from Her children that She spoke to him. Her voice was emotion, the music of Her womb.

Through his misery, he reached out to Her with his tiny, lonely soul and cried for Her to lift him, hold him, cradle him to Her neck and let him safely exist in the scent of Her breath and the pulsing of Her heart.

Parts of him faltered when the blade parted the skin in his tenderest areas, but he forced it down. Denied it. No physical pain could compare with that of a loving Mother forever separated from her babies. He would endure his. This pain was transformation. Ascendancy. Apotheosis.

Isobel, face stained brown and red with drying blood, held his cheeks in her gooey hands and kissed his lips. She wore her empathy without shame. Rivers of tears crept from her beautiful brown eyes and cut through the blood on her face, dripping pink onto the chest of her lab coat. As painful as releasing him was for her, he knew she understood. Just as Thalia had told him before, this performance, this small sacrifice, was an act of purest love.

She took his mask last. Stretching and peeling the neck. Separating the ears, one at a time. Slicing away the jelly lips. The crunch of steel dragging across bone groaned in his ears and vibrated his molars. Fluid filled his ear holes, amplifying the steady pulsing of blood whooshing through his body. Wetness coursed down the last of his nerves as blood dribbled off his eyelids, hiding the clouds behind a veil of pink, red, and purple.

The moment the last of his shell was clipped away with the tip of his nose, the itching and the pain ceased. His soul awakened, and he cried for Her, voiceless and sorrowful. Cried out with his soul. Screamed his terror and fear into the clouds, letting his light flow from him until the last few drops of his life force clung to him, knowing that if they let go, if his agony ended too soon, She wouldn't find them.

He wished he could move. Follow the string of his heart and stretch himself past the atmosphere to curl and weave among the stars. If he could only have at least a moment to see more clearly or blink away the blood staining daylight.

Lance pushed aside any thoughts of regret as he watched everyone transform through Mother's heavenly power.

Isobel stood stunned, chin tilted to the sky, lips peeling upward and tearing past the gumline, her gaping maw and widened eyes paralyzed in a moment of pure ecstasy as the sky split open to reveal giant tentacles of magenta energy curling through the clouds and pulling a star-filled sphere of burning darkness below the atmosphere.

Thalia, too, had her cage split under her nail bed and slowly stripped away until it sloshed at her feet. All the others followed suit, forsaking their barriers with silent screams toward the sky.

Shrieks of fear battered the air above the streets below. Other people, the ones who didn't know or couldn't remember how separated from Her, called to Her. They screeched their terror like trumpets blasting upward, their pain and fear being sucked from them by a power they forgot existed.

Lance's permanent smile widened. They may not

know their mistakes, but they would understand, just as he understood. Soon, they'd give away their shells, too, peel away the sticky rind that kept them from feeling Her love. Because She had returned.

Mother had finally come home.

About the Author

J.E. Erickson fell in love with horror and fantasy at an early age. The first story he wrote was at age 11 and was about a child walking home from school to discover his own gravestone. He still thinks about it when referring to himself in third person.

He currently writes horror and fantasy stories, and lives in an old house in the Midwestern United States with a nerdy soap maker, two spoiled dogs, and a (potentially) possessed vegetable garden.

You can visit him at jeericksonwriting.com, on Twitter @maladjustined, and Instagram @j.e.erickson

www.ingramcontent.com/pod-product-compliance
Lightning Source LLC
Chambersburg PA
CBHW021114130726
47988CB00003B/1016